LOVED BY LOVE

"Excited for Maritza's journey with the Lord to help propel you further into yours. We have personally witnessed her love for Jesus and for those around her. Let the testimony of Jesus in her life be multiplied into yours."

– Aaron and Beth Packard, Firestorm International

"Maritza writes about challenges that so many of us face in life. She is audacious to solve these with seemingly simple solutions as commands from the Bible that most people have difficulty grasping. She will take you on a journey of the battlefield within her mind and life to discover where the solution lies. I love Maritza's transparency and her willingness to share her deepest troubles in order to help us ALL experience freedom. God wants us to live free, and the theme of this book will help you achieve it."

– Bob Donnelly, Tetelestai Ministries

"We all have one life to live and to live it to the fullest. We are all on a journey of discovery and growth. While Maritza's journey is specific to her, in this raw collection of her life's testimonies you will see what growth, strength, and realization of relying on the truth really looks like. Once you read this, you too will see that we are all faced with different challenges and obstacles, yet it is our choice to submit to God, resist the enemy and then the enemy will flee. From there we draw near to God, and He will draw near to us which makes the healing process that much sweeter. It is in these moments that our belief systems are reinforced, reshaped, or sharpened. James 4:7-8 states "Therefore submit to God. Resist the devil and he will flee from you. Draw near to God and He will draw near to you. Cleanse *your* hands, *you* sinners;   and purify *your* hearts, *you* double-minded."

– Kimberly Ennis, Pastor/Director Roar House Ministry and Healing Rooms

ISBN: 9780578331065

Unless otherwise identified, all Scripture quotations are taken
from the Holman Christian Standard Bible (HCSB) © 2011 By
Holman Bible Publishers

Scripture taken from International Children's Bible (ICB).
© 2021 by Thomas Nelson

Scripture taken from the Berean Study Bible (BSB). © 2016 by
the Bible Hub. www.Biblehub.com

Scripture taken from New King James Version (NKJV). © 2015
by Thomas Nelson, Inc.

Scripture taken from King James Version (KJV). © 1934 by
Frank Charles Thompson

First Printing, 2021

Loved By Love

How Love Restores a Heart

MARITZA BARRON

Maritza Barron

I would like to dedicate this book to the God of Love; Father, Son and Holy Spirit. Thank you for loving me, pursuing me, and making me your own. Your Love is life itself to me. I love you.

Acknowledgements

I'd like to acknowledge those who have encouraged me and believed in me. Tracy Taylor and Vanessa Sánchez, thank you for your patience and belief in me.

Beth Packard, thank you for allowing me to call you, text you and come to you for prayer and encouragement.

Antoinette, thank you for your help. There were others, you know exactly who you are. I truly appreciate each one of you. Without you, I may have never gotten this out.

Contents

Contents

Forward

By Scott McNamara

The signature of this book is hope.

With candid vulnerability, Maritza writes from the heart bravely, not afraid to re-visit some of her most personal and painful experiences to allow the reader to find healing from their own despair. She interweaves her own story, weightily supported by the strength of scripture to beautifully provide a solution and a way out of any such problems at every juncture.

Revealing clearly that love, specifically God's love for us, is the divine antidote to our poisoned hearts.

The hand of God's love knows no limitations regardless of the severity to which we've been marred. He is the potter who can fix and rebuild even the worst cracked and broken vessels.

Scott McNamara, Founder
Jesus at the Door

Introduction

"Does love *really* conquer all? Does love *really* overcome bad? Is Love even *real*? Does it even exist???"

I found myself vocalizing these questions while in my room, my eyes swollen with tears. I had a deep desire to see things turn around from bad to good in my life, and to see my life hold significance in this world. I needed to know that love truly existed and that my life mattered to someone, yet I felt so lost and unwanted.

Here I was, feeling hopeless, small and forsaken on the day I cried out these questions deep in my soul. Have you ever felt this way, too?

I longed to know that I mattered, that someone out there loved me. I wanted to be loved and to feel loved; to experience real love.

This is exactly the point I had reached on a day in September 2015, when I began my search for answers, and what began my faith walk, my love story.

You see, I grew up believing that God existed, yet never knew who this God was or how real He really is. These questions I asked had come from a place deep down in the core of my being, and God was so faithful to answer me. He took me on this journey that I am about to share with you. It is a journey of finding real love which led to a journey of finding myself, a journey of finding what love really is, or rather *Who* Love really is.

It is a story of what Love can do. How love can take a heart that has been wounded through loss, pain, hurt, trauma, betrayal, and circumstances in this battle we call "life," and restore it.

In essence it is a story of a heart being restored to life full of hope, joy and wonder.

If you are in a place where I was that day, and are asking questions like I was, I invite you to continue reading. If you are feeling hopeless, small, and forsaken, this story is for you. If you battle with bitterness, anger, and frustration, this is for you. If you feel lost, unloved, unwanted, rejected, fearful, alone, worthless, disappointed even to the point of having a death wish, this is for you. I ENCOURAGE you to turn the page and keep on reading. Love is calling you.

Chapter 1

So It Begins

"You meant to hurt me. But God turned your evil into good. It was to save the lives of many people. And it is being done." Genesis 50:20 (ICB)

The minute you were born, you came into this life with a purpose, you were created on purpose for a purpose. You are not a mistake; you have been created for great things and to live an extraordinary life.

As you read this, you may be thinking that you are far from living an extraordinary life. In fact, you may feel that you are only existing or just merely surviving.

I have news for you, there are things that have been holding you back, things you are unable to explain, or understand, or even pinpoint. You feel it, but you don't know what has been holding you back from this extraordinary life—a life full of joy, hope, and love which you were created for. I am here not only to expose what has been holding you back, but also to share how Love itself has come to restore this life that you are meant to have. I am also here to tell you that you are fully loved and that you are not too far gone.

I will share things about my life so that you might understand what some of the things were that worked against me. They may be similar to what might be working against you and keeping you from your destiny and from living an extraordinary life. Let your eyes and heart open so that you may be set free of the things that are holding you back. I want to share this journey of mine so that you may come to see how Love came in to give me life, and that you may also know that Love is knocking at the door of your heart.

Belong and Seen

As a child, for the most part I remember being surrounded by people. Every weekend we were either at a family gathering, or a party. I realize this produced a sense of being overlooked, being lost in the crowd somewhere, always blending in, feeling hidden.

I was born in Southern California and later would move to Portland Oregon. I grew up with three siblings up until the age of 10 which is when my fourth sibling was born. I became the middle child, and once again, I felt lost even amongst my family. Here at such an early age, the desire to be seen began to sprout which would carry into adulthood.

Belonging. This is another desire that was planted in me as a child, one that grew more and more as I got older. See, as a child, I looked different from most of my family. I don't want to imply that my appearance was everything back then or even now, but this became something that the enemy of our souls used to make me feel "less than" and to make me feel that I didn't belong. He succeeded for a very long time.

This enemy—the enemy of our souls, the father of lies—comes to steal, kill, and destroy, and surely, he came in at a very young age to do exactly that with my life. I explain this so that you might understand that all I had experienced is not to be blamed on any person, I just want to make that VERY CLEAR. There is more than the eye can see. Actually, the Bible tells us that *"our battle is not against flesh and blood but against the rulers, against the authorities, against the world powers of this darkness, against the spiritual forces of evil in the heavens."* Ephesians 6:12. When we read that scripture again, we notice that our battle takes place in the unseen. We should understand that in this world, we have an invisible enemy that is against our very life, and unfortunately this enemy sometimes uses people—even well-meaning people we love—to hurt us.

This would be the case for me. People I loved were the ones used against me regarding my appearance. The first element I felt rejected for was my skin color. When I was young, I was a few shades darker than anyone in my sphere. I was different, I stood out, so I would hear nicknames that I particularly didn't like and would be told that I was adopted, amongst other hurtful comments. As you can imagine as a child, this created many wounds in my heart, wounds I didn't know were there until later in life.

To add to this, at the age of 8, my parents moved our family to the Portland area in 1995, from Southern California. I would be one of few Hispanic children in my school for both elementary and middle school where again, I was unmistakably different, making me feel that I didn't belong. I also remember being told that because my skin was darker, I was ugly. All these experiences led me to feel rejected in the Mexican culture along with the American culture, and eventually it led me to feel rejected altogether. The word "ugly" began to distort my view of how I saw myself, and I believed it.

I am extremely sad to admit, but up until my late twenties I hated my skin color, and I also hated my hair because it, too, was different from my family's. Let me get real, I could easily say that I hated how I looked. I often would meet people who told me how beautiful I am and they would tell me that my skin color was gorgeous, but the belief of being ugly was so strong in me that it was hard to believe what they said.

I really tried "brushing this off" but it was hard. I'd say it was near impossible. I also want to emphasize that the old adage we learn in school "sticks and stones will break my bones but words can never hurt me," is one of the biggest lies ever told. I think I would rather have had my arm or leg broken than to have gone through what I experienced feeling ugly and rejected. Nevertheless, I now have been able to unmask the lies that I had believed and struggled with, and I am hoping that my story will help you do the same.

More Wounds

As if that wasn't enough for a child to take in, the enemy indeed went further. One summer as an 8-year-old, I was sexually molested. No child should ever have to go through that. No person should have to go through that. If this has been you, please know that my heart goes out to you.

I felt such shame and fear, I didn't know what to do, I didn't tell anyone. A year later, another man started touching my legs inappropriately. This time, before any more damage could be done, I told my mom as soon as I saw her, and we never saw that man in our lives again. This would be a starting point in my life when subconsciously I decided that I did not trust the opposite sex. I didn't realize until later in life that I had made this decision. But my inner being had been blemished and my heart wounded. Fear came in along with more pain and more shame and made themselves at home in my heart which had been lying dormant for the opportune moment.

The damage was done, and to reverse all these wounds would only become possible by the One who created me (and the same can be done for you). This was a healing process that also involved "rewiring" my brain as an adult using a variety of resources like an amazing program from Dr. Caroline Leaf called "21 Day Detox", along with oh so many "God moments" and prayers when I continuously looked for the Truth of what God has said about me. Praise God for Holy Spirit who tells us Truth. I will share more on this later.

God Turns all into Good

"You meant to hurt me. But God turned your evil into good. It was to save the lives of many people. And it is being done." Genesis 50:20 (ICB)

Before we move forward, if you are new to anything that has to do with God, if you have not heard of Jesus, please believe that this scripture is so true. The planned evil is all from the enemy that I briefly mentioned earlier who is also known as the father of lies, the devil. Here is Truth: everything that the enemy does, God turns it for good.

From childhood into adulthood, this enemy was sneaky, causing havoc in my heart. This caused me to be in a very low place in life until I encountered the Love of God, or should I say when I encountered Love himself. I came to learn that *God is Love* (1 John 4:8), and He is the

One who has already overcome this enemy and is ready and willing to help us get our life back.

The best part about Genesis 50:20 is where it says, *"God turned it for good to save the lives of many people."* I can wholeheartedly say that God has used every situation in my life, not just for my good, but for me to be able to share my story with others for their own good, so that they may live and have hope again.

Are you in a place right now where others have said things to you, or experienced circumstances that have caused your heart to be wounded? If so, I want to share another scripture with you, *"The thief comes only to steal and kill and destroy. I have come that they may have life, and have it in all its fullness."* John 10:10 Berean Study Bible. I am sharing my story with you so that you may know that the enemy is a thief trying to steal your life just as he did mine, but Jesus is here and He is the only One who can redeem it, in fact He already has.

Chapter 2

Dreams Deferred

"Hope deferred makes the heart sick, But when the desire comes, it is a tree of life" Proverbs 13:12 (NKJV)

Dreams. Those dreams that pull on your heart that bring such joy to talk about, those are dreams that God put in you. They are for walking out your purpose and destiny. Hear me on this because these dreams play a huge role in your life. However, this is another area that the enemy can cause more wounds in your heart, which is why I believe it to be crucial for me to share how my dreams were used to come against my joy.

Dreams are meant for helping us live a life of abundance and joy. A small example of this for me is I remember writing down "impact lives", even though I honestly didn't have a clear idea of how this dream would unfold. Today, I find myself writing and have heard many people say that my writing positively impacts them. Growing up, I never liked writing—in fact, I failed Writing-121 in college and had to retake it! Yet writing is a method God chose for me to impact lives.

I would like to think that I am not the only dreamer in this world. Though I will admit that for a long time, I was one of the biggest dreamers I knew in my sphere. I was the person people made fun of since I had huge dreams. They would say to me, "You think money grows on trees." My dreams to some seemed as wishful daydreams, and to others as me just being selfish. I recently told a friend of mine that if your dreams tug on your heart and you see yourself making a difference with them, more than likely these are the ones meant to send you into your life destiny.

I had a mentor tell me, "If your dream doesn't scare you, it is not big enough." Well, that wasn't me. My dreams scared me because I had no means to get there. Some of these dreams involved getting married, having children, traveling the world, building non-profits of some sort, having a big home with a ginormous kitchen (which, of course, I would only use for baking because I don't like to cook! I enjoy gathering people, and the kitchen is where the most connection happens in a home, over food). I also wanted to be able to give financially to different organizations. I was in a place in my life where I wanted to give and give, but I didn't really have much to give, (or so I thought).

Here is another way that my dreams came against me: I had "planned my life" where I put a timeline on when I felt certain dreams and events needed to happen by. I am certain that I am not the only one guilty here. **And let me tell you that if you are still planning your life and trying to control everything in your life, this will bring unnecessary stress, unnecessary worries, and possibly unnecessary diseases or ailments.**

I am aware that society tells us to plan the future, but God says, *"Therefore don't worry about tomorrow, because tomorrow will worry about itself. Each day has enough trouble of its own."* Matthew 6:34. This is the very last verse in a chapter of scripture titled "The Cure for Anxiety" in my Holman Christian Standard Bible. We should take a hint. Personally, I didn't know this truth until later in life, which is why I had such unrest in my soul.

The following is the biggest and deepest dream that I had, which in my mind, would be the end of myself and the beginning of something new. It was the thing that I felt would determine my worth—the thing that I felt would complete me and bring me all the happiness in the world. I felt it was the *most* important thing in my life. This dream was for me to be married.

When I was in high school, I had planned to go to college, meet someone, and be a stay-at-home mom. I never planned on a career. I can now laugh at this, but I promise it was not funny back then. I had made up my mind back then that I wanted to get married and have children by the age of 27. I am now 33, unmarried, and have no children. When I turned 27, fears started churning in my heart. Anxieties started to emerge, emotions that were suppressed began to rise up, painful issues that I had been completely unaware of were thrust into my daily reality. The rejection that had begun in childhood began to rear its ugly head. I began hearing lies in my head that I was "unwanted", that I was "ugly", that I was "not good enough" and that I was "not worthy". I even began hearing new insults like, I was "not smart enough." I began feeling a fear that became far too real to me. I will share more about this fear in a later chapter.

I would have thought that by the time I had reached the age of 27, I would have had *something* materialize from my dreams and plans. But not a single thing had come to fruition at this point. Disappointment took root in my heart. The feeling of being a failure commenced, and on top of that, I was still living with family which caused a sense of worthlessness in society. I felt as if I were nothing, and going nowhere fast.

There is Still Hope

Can you relate? If you are in a place where you feel that you are nothing, that you have completely failed, or that you are not successful in anything, I am here to tell you that there is still hope!

Reread the scripture at the beginning of this chapter: *"Hope deferred makes the heart sick, But when the desire comes, it is a tree of life."* Proverbs 13:12 (NKJV)

Better yet, I will also give you a different translation of it. *"Delayed hope makes the heart sick, But fulfilled desire is a tree of life."* Proverbs 13:12 (HCSB) There is a KEY word here! Delayed – or deferred.

The Vine's Complete Expository Dictionary breaks down the word "delay" as coming from two Greek words. One of these is a root word for "time" and it means "to while away time" and "tarried, tarried so long."

Now, the word *tarry – or tarried –* has over ten Greek root words. One of these words means "to expect, await" and "to receive". Another definition of tarry that we should notice is "to abide still, continue, suggesting patience and steadfastness in remaining after the circumstances which preceded." What this means to us is—in our waiting moments, time may seem to be wasting away, but it is not. What this speaks of is that while we are in waiting, we remain patient in expectation, ready to receive. This is *truly* the meaning of "delay". Something will still come to pass, but it will occur a bit later than what we originally thought; so we remain, and we remain expectant, with great joy.

Brother, sister, you are not a failure, you are not unwanted, you are not overlooked or forsaken. The hopes and dreams that have been placed in your heart by God himself are just on a *delay*. Your journey isn't over for you. It also means that your plans are not His plans. If your life does not look the way you always thought it would, it simply means that God has a different plan, and something *better*! Something that will completely bring the joy and the fulfillment in your heart that will produce a tree of life. The only thing is we need to be willing to surrender these things to Him and to His timing. When we surrender and choose to trust God, the dreams placed in our heart by Him will come to fruition. They may not happen when we want them to, or they may not even look like how we imagined them. Don't give up on your dreams, press in to the One who has planted them in your heart.

I hear you say, "Well Maritza, you told us you're not married yet. What do you mean desire will be fulfilled, what do you mean there is still hope? How can you say that?"

Oh, I am SO GLAD you asked! Keep on turning the page.

Chapter 3

Anchor To My Soul

"This hope we have as an anchor of the soul, both sure and steadfast, and which enters the Presence behind the veil." Hebrews 6:19 (NKJV)

As I reflected on my life and began to write this book, I asked myself, "What kept me continuing to seek God?" Please understand, I believe it could have been so easy for me to give up on life because of things I experienced as a child. Walking through rejection and major disappointment felt as if God was non-existent. So, what kept me going? Recently, as I was reading Hebrews 6:19, it hit me! I want to repeat this scripture *"This hope we have as an anchor of the soul, both sure and steadfast, and which enters the Presence behind the veil."* Hebrews 6:19 NKJV. What had kept me seeking and kept me moving forward and not giving up was the power and strength of the Holy Spirit.

Growing up, I was not taught about Holy Spirit. Holy Spirit back then was more like "He is there but we don't talk about Holy Spirit." Quite honestly, all I knew about Holy Spirit was that we would mention "Holy Spirit" as we did the "sign of the cross" in the church that I went to. I knew He was part of the Trinity and that's all. In Truth, Holy Spirit is someone everyone should come to know. Holy Spirit is just as important as the Father and the Son. The truth is, without Holy Spirit, we are unable to live a supernatural life that we are called to live, an extraordinary life that we were created for. At this point, you may be wondering "Who is this Holy Spirit?" I will explain later in this chapter.

Filled with the Holy Ghost

In 2014, a particular day became one of blessing for me. God let down an anchor from the heavenlies into my soul which would keep me from drifting away and keep me holding on in spite of my turmoil that would come later. Up to this point, I was still oblivious and unaware of the spiritual war against our lives. However, in May of 2014, I had a wonderful experience that became a marking point in my life and an important step in my journey in dealing with the spiritual war against me.

I was 26 years old at the time when I had been invited to a church by a coworker and began attending nearly every Sunday for about six months. Sometime in April, there was an announcement made in church about a women's conference coming up in May. The thought of attending didn't enter my mind as I felt that I had more important things to do. In my opinion, attending this conference didn't even deserve a thought. During the weeks that followed the announcement, my co-worker's wife invited me several times to attend, and it was hard for me to say no to her since she was so full of hope and excitement! Shaking my head I laugh now, because at the time, I was very resistant to committing myself to attend events pertaining to God, though ironically my heart really wanted to learn. I wonder if you can relate? Have you, too, found yourself resisting His nudges? If so, I understand. As you can see, I have been there. Just know that God is patient.

The entire women's conference was going to take place over three full days. When my resistance to attending finally broke and I had said yes to this loving persistent woman, I said, "Okay, but I can only make it one night." You see, in that moment, I made a decision to schedule plans during the other two evening sessions of the conference so that I wouldn't be outright lying to her. I would be working during the day, and then I purposely booked appointments for the other two evenings so that I would be completely unavailable to attend the full conference. I also never moved a finger to schedule time off from work. My priority was work and not the Kingdom of Heaven. But Praise God that His priority during this time was *me*! I share about my resistance and purposely booking my calendar to avoid the conference because I wonder if some of you might be doing similar things.

So on May 21, 2014, at 7 pm., I attended the evening session of the women's conference. Unbeknownst to me, this would be a day that marked my life. A day that I would be sealed for life for God. A day in which I received an anchor for my soul that would forever keep me secure, even when I didn't know it or perceive it. This anchor guided me and helped me in times when I have needed it most. And even now as I write this, I have the 20-20 hindsight to say this with confidence.

I remember that the Pastor spoke on the book of Ephesians—a book in the Bible that would later become not only my favorite, but also my source for knowing my true identity and for creating a standard in my life. Incidentally, it was later this same year that I had purchased my first Bible. Personally, I had never read the Bible prior to this as I wasn't taught the importance of it.

What I heard the night of this conference was quite new for me, but it made my spirit jump with excitement. That night, she spoke about the spiritual warfare and the power of Holy Spirit, which I had never heard about before. That evening I also heard that Holy Spirit has a role in the God Head, and I heard about Holy Spirit having wonderful attributes. For example, I heard that Holy Spirit is our comforter, and that Holy Spirit intercedes for us when we don't know what to pray, yet our spirit does. *"In the same way the Spirit also joins to help our weakness, because we do not know what to pray for as we should but the spirit Himself intercedes for us with unspoken groanings."* Romans 8:26. Knowing Holy Spirit now is beyond anything I could have imagined. At the time, I had no idea that I was certainly in for an ultimate ride of adventure that I did not expect. This ultimate adventure is also for you and waiting for you to take the leap of faith and believe.

What happened after the teaching was by far the most important thing ever in my life. It is what marked me forever; it is probably as important as me being born. I was sitting towards the back of the sanctuary among the congregation of women. I recall a question asked by the pastor. She asked, "Who here wants to have the power of the Holy Spirit?" Before I could even think about the question, I found myself walking towards the altar with a crowd of other women. As I was walking, all I can remember thinking was, "What am I doing?", followed by, "Why not have that power she spoke of?"

I went to the altar along with what seemed to be about fifty other women who were lined up shoulder to shoulder in front of the altar. The Pastor gave us one piece of advice which was simply to open our mouths and speak. She recommended that we select a word to repeat and focus on, and then she began laying her hands on each woman and prayed over us. My word of choice was "Glory."

There I was, repeating the word "Glory" as in intentional invitation for God to encounter me, when the pastor reached me and laid her hands in prayer on me. My eyes were closed and somehow my tongue started feeling like I was unable to control it, and utterances that I do not know what they meant started to come out of my mouth. I had begun to pray in the spirit, or as others may understand it to be called—to speak in tongues. It felt like it was coming from the depths of my being, something not from myself or from my own thoughts. It was strong. Suddenly at one point, I felt the pastor standing in front of me and she spoke into the microphone saying, "The Lord really has ahold of this one!" I stopped my uttering and realized that I was unable to open my eyes. I told her, "I hear you, but I cannot open my eyes." Then she told me that it was ok and not to worry about it. As I stood there praying in tongues, I began begging God to allow me to open my eyes. He heard me because shortly after I was able to open them. When I looked around, I was the only one left at the altar. I turned around to return to my seat, avoiding eye contact with anyone, feeling a little embarrassed. I was embarrassed because I still did not understand. As I look back now, I can see that in that moment, God was showing me that I had a unique calling that He was preparing me for.

This was my "baptism" of the Holy Spirit. Holy Spirit became my hope that "came in behind the curtain" as the scripture says, in the deepest place of my heart, and has kept me anchored—anchored during the storms of my life.

Holy Spirit Is Real

As I mentioned that prior to this event, I didn't know that Holy Spirit was real. I didn't know that Holy Spirit, being part of the Trinity, was One who I could invite into my life or who could help me. You may be in the same place where, like me, you might have heard of Holy Spirit yet not know much about Him. Or maybe you have never heard of Holy Spirit and this is your first time hearing about Him. Regardless, I am here to share that Holy Spirit is real.

There are a few names for Holy Spirt such as Counselor, Comforter, Spirit of Truth (John 14:17), Helper, Intercessor, Advocate. You will find these names used for Him depending on the various translations of the Bible you are using. Some specific scriptures are John 14:26, John 16:7, John 15:26. There is also 1 Corinthians 12:8-10 which describes the gifts of Holy Spirit.

We also learn about the fruit of the Holy Spirit in Galatians 5:22 *"But the fruit of the Spirit is LOVE, joy, peace, patience, kindness. Goodness, faith, gentleness, self-control."* Who wouldn't want these fruits in life? Personally, I want all of them, and with Holy Spirit these are all available now while we are here on earth.

Receive the Baptism of the Holy Spirit

If you have not yet been baptized with Holy Spirit, ask Holy Spirit to come into your life. This baptism is something that we are allowed to ask for. Some may believe that this baptism will come upon them only "if" God wants to give this gift to us and only "if" God wants us to receive it. Seriously? The Holy Spirit wants all of us to know Him and to be speaking in tongues, which is our heavenly language. It is a gift of the Holy Spirit. It is a gift, freely given to those who receive. Luke 11:13 says, *"If you then, who are evil, know how to give good gifts to your children, how much more will the heavenly Father give the Holy Spirit to those who ask Him?"* Also, scripture tells us we should desire the gifts: *"Pursue love and desire spiritual gifts, and above all that you may prophesy."* 1 Corinthians 14:1.

If you are wanting to be baptized with the Holy Spirit with the evidence of speaking in tongues, you can do this now. First you will need to believe in Jesus for you to receive Holy Spirit, and then ask for it. If you have asked before and it hasn't happened for you, there might be something that is hindering it from coming to you. I do know of one thing for sure that will block this. Bitterness. If you have any bitterness in your heart, this may be preventing the fullness of that baptism.

When I was filled with the Holy Spirit and started speaking in tongues, it was before I had fully surrendered every part of my life over to the Lord. As I look back, I realize that I cannot recall an actual point in time when I became "saved"* prior to my experience with Holy Spirit, but I was certainly searching for God, and had begun to some degree to believe in Jesus. Therefore, if the Lord freely gave this gift of the baptism of the Holy Spirit to me at that time in my life, what would prevent someone else from receiving this wonderful gift? I read something one day that made everything clear to me. "No person can be baptized with the Holy Spirit and have bitterness, that is, gall" in _Smith Wigglesworth on the Holy Spirit_. We are to have a heart free of bitterness which is what makes a heart a dwelling home for the Holy Spirit.

I can conclude that when this encounter happened for me, I had no bitterness in my heart which is why I was able to receive. So even at this moment, if you want the baptism of the Holy Spirit and you have bitterness in your heart, repent, bring it to God, forgive the people that have hurt you; it is only holding you captive, not them. If the person you need to forgive is yourself, please forgive yourself. I realize that forgiving ourselves is one of the hardest things to do, but it is extremely important that you do this. I have had to do this, so believe me when I say that I know that it is hard. Anything you have done, Jesus has taken it on the cross, even the shame and embarrassment. The unforgiveness and bitterness is keeping you from this beautiful gift and friend called Holy Spirit. This friend that will give you a dynamic life, and extraordinary life.

***If you need a jump-start to forgiving yourself, you will find this at the back of this book under Forgiveness.

*Saved: believe and trust that Jesus sacrificed his life for us so that we can have open access to God and experience a full relationship with Him – Romans 3:23-26

Chapter 4

Gripped By Fear

"The fear of man is a snare, but the one who trusts in the LORD is protected." Proverbs 29:25 (HCSB)

In case that verse doesn't sink in let's try these verses of a song from Zach Williams.

"Fear, he is a liar
He will take your breath
Stop you in your steps
Fear, he is a liar
He will rob your rest
Steal your happiness
Cast your fear in the fire
'Cause fear, he is a liar"

In May of 2014, at the women's conference, I had experienced my encounter with God just as the disciples did in the second chapter of the book of Acts in the Bible. I, Maritza Barron, was filled with Holy Spirit and speaking in tongues like flames of fire. Holy Spirit had personally come to me.

Unfortunately at the time, I did not know just how remarkable this was, having grown up in a religious tradition that did not teach about Holy Spirit. Without a doubt, I knew deep down that my experience had been a good thing; certainly one of God's mysteries. But at this point of my journey, I did not yet have anyone that would take me under their wing, or mentor me and help me understand what had taken place and what kind of power was within me. I mentioned in the beginning of this book that our fight is not against flesh and blood. The adversary, which is the devil, is one with whom we fight—the enemy of our soul who goes about like a prowling lion seeing who he can devour. He saw something vulnerable in me that I did not realize, and he was about to attack. And attack he did.

One thing is certain at this point in my journey is that my heart longed to know God. I began listening to Sunday services from a church online that fed my soul during my Sunday morning run. I was still so new to this whole "God" concept, and as you know, even though I had purchased my first Bible, I hadn't yet understood the importance of reading it and staying in God's Word.

Another point I want to share to encourage you is that if you have ever been hurt by anyone in a church, don't use that as an excuse to stop pursuing Jesus. Jesus will never ever condemn you or leave you. I say this because the reason I listened to online church services instead of continuing to go to church is that I had been hurt and felt judged where I had been attending. **Here is a brief tip: we should never blame God for the behavior of man; we are the ones to lose many blessings otherwise.**

I knew that this hurtful situation wasn't of God and I sincerely wanted to seek His face and have Him teach me. I am thankful that I did not let that stop me from pursuing Truth. My morning runs with the Sunday messages were awesome, I loved it! But I didn't realize at the time that I needed connection with others that would help me stay on course with God and help keep me accountable.

At this time, I had just turned 27—the notorious age by which I had decided I should have certain achievements and accomplishments. The age by when I thought I would have had a husband and some children—these were my greatest desires. I was still searching for what I thought was love. I was getting desperate and unsettled in my heart. I still wanted to be loved and to be cared about, to have a life of adventure that I would share with someone who I truly connected with.

I had gone out on a few dates, but for some reason it never went past the first or second date. I could not understand why. It was hurtful to experience rejection or no call backs. I did have an idea that it was mostly due to my views on premarital sex. I was not going to have sex before marriage, that was my decision from an early age. I had grown up with a desire to wait until marriage and because of that, I had to experience (many times over) men finding this out and then losing interest and moving on.

I allowed fear to truly enter my heart. I was panicking. Keep in mind that an expectation as a Mexican is that you get married and have children by a certain age, usually mid-twenties, otherwise you are "just too old". I was now passed that age. I could hear what the family was saying. Internally, I would beat myself up about this, and slowly I started to hate myself, to hate the dreamer in me, to hate the self-control in me, to hate my desires of righteousness and of being good. I didn't notice this taking place, but it began to take root. I had seen my twin brother marry when we were both 25, and they had a baby by the time we were 26. I was happy for him, but I also thought, "What about me?" My own expectations and the expectations that others had of me began to cage me up with fear. Fear was speaking into my heart and soul. This is when the enemy saw the opportunity to strike!

I met a guy at one of my favorites hangouts where I had often gone to study during my last term in college. This young man was amiable and seemed hard working – what every woman wants, right?! This particular evening of the week happened to be when motorcyclists would come to gather. There he was with his motorcycle, and what I saw in him was adventure; it is what my heart wanted. After awhile, I walked over to him to say hello. Since I was somewhat familiar with motorcycles from working at the bank where we offered motorcycle loans, I knew enough to strike up a conversation with him. After talking for several minutes, he asked me for my number and asked me on a date.

We seemed to have so much in common. I even found out that he was a dreamer and this by far is what made me most excited! I longed to meet someone who had dreams for the future. On the day of our date, right before he came to pick me up, a thought hit me out of nowhere! "What if he expects to have sex?!" I started panicking and asked God for help. At this point of my journey with God, even though I had experienced being filled with Holy Spirit the year prior, I still did not understand yet whether or not God heard my prayers, my cries, or pleas for help. I had absolutely no idea if He did or didn't, yet I asked for strength.

Later that evening, I discovered that the subtle voice that had come as a thought prior to the date was for good reason. Holy Spirit, as a small voice in my being, wanted me to be prepared. Indeed, this guy wanted to have sex. I had the boldness to say no, and sure enough after I said no, he took me home.

That night I laid in bed crying. Mentally I started beating myself up because in my mind, I was the one to blame for the rejection. The thoughts in my head were so loud, "I am a complete fool, an idiot, stupid and naïve." These thoughts were running through my head on replay, and as they did, more self-hatred grew – hatred for the childlike faith and the innocence and purity in me.

What pushed me over the edge was hearing, *"You have been rejected your whole life by men up until now. What if you turn 30 years old and you're still a virgin? What man is going to want you? No man will want you. Who would want an inexperienced girl?"*

My heart was completely gripped with fear. It was a sandwich of fear—my past and my future full of rejection. I was convinced that I would never be wanted. I ate that sandwich up like no tomorrow and choked on it.

Fear had now become greater than my desires, than my beliefs, than my convictions, than anything I had ever known. All I could see, feel, think, smell, and taste was fear. What happened next, after a few days of continually dwelling in this fear, was done with clear motives and intentions on my part. Intentions to move forward with this young man's original expectation of me because I did not want to live with this rejection any longer. The decision was made and that was that. I sent a message to him letting him know that I really wanted to meet up with him again.

And we did.

Before I go on, I want to stop here and just briefly mention. I don't know what your beliefs are about sex outside of marriage, but Truth is that doing so goes against God's will.

When we have sex outside of the covenant of marriage, our souls become fragmented.

Scripture says that we become one with the other person when we have sex with them. This causes our souls to then be attached to that person. Having sex outside of the covenant of marriage brings inner turmoil to our soul, and this is another way that the enemy causes wounds and confusion in our hearts.

Entangled in the Snare

Fear had taken the best of me.

"Fear, he is a liar
He will take your breath
Stop you in your steps
Fear, he is a liar
He will rob your rest
Steal your happiness
Cast your fear in the fire
'Cause fear, he is a liar"

Fear took my breath, fear took my rest, and fear stole my happiness. By seeing that guy again, I answered to fear instead of trusting in God. I did the very thing with him that went against my beliefs because of fear shaking me to the very core of my being. Instead of realizing this lie, I opened the door to shame, guilt, doubt, self-hatred, anger and more bitterness—and no surprise, the rejection never left. As soon as the deed was done, I felt numb, I felt dead. That happiness I longed for and the joy I wanted was nowhere to be found. This is just one example of the many things that fear can do. It will tell you lies straight from the pit of hell. These lies will choke out Truth of who we really are and take away all the beauty that life has for us. Even though I quickly turned back to God asking for forgiveness, I still hadn't put my trust in the Lord in all things, and fear was now making its home in me and taking up a throne in my heart.

The fear you might also be feeling, the fear you are possibly dealing with, might be different from what I was experiencing, or it might be the same. Fear can take hold as a fear of rejection, fear of failure, fear of disappointment, fear of the future, or fear of the unknown, just to name a few. I had let all those fears come into my life, and let me tell you, fear *cannot* dwell in the *same* place as Love. Fear literally will kill us in life, it only brings death.

But Love gives us life! It already has, Love has come, and his name is Jesus. He says He *"came to give us life and give it to us to the fullest."* John 10:10. So, if you have any fear in your life right now, my friend, I silence every lie over you in the mighty name of Jesus and I speak life over you right now this very minute.

Chapter 5

Crying Out

"You will seek Me and find Me when you search for Me with all your heart." Jeremiah 29:13 (HCSB)

I had reached a new low after allowing myself to participate in things that had gone against my beliefs and values, and I was shaken to the core. On an evening in September 2015, fallen to my knees, my eyes swollen with tears, there I was on the floor, crying out my questions "Does love *really* conquer all? Does love *really* overcome bad? Is Love even *real*? Does it even exist???"

I had always held on to the belief that love was real. I wanted so desperately to see that my own life had significance in this world and to see that love truly existed. Yet here I was, feeling so lost, so hopeless, small, and forsaken. This might be a place that you, too, have experienced or might be experiencing now.

I promise you, you are *not* forsaken.

I didn't know this to be true back then. In time, I would come across a scripture in God's word that says,

"Be strong and courageous. Do not be terrified or afraid of them. For it is the Lord your God who goes with you; He will not leave you or forsake you." Deuteronomy 31:6. God created you and you are His child, and He will never leave His child behind, He is always near and ready to help.

Personal God

Feeling desperately confused and alone, I knew deep down that there had to be more to life—that I had to be here for a reason, but I just couldn't see any reason anymore. Here I was with too many regrets full of "should've." This should have happened by now, that should have happened by now. Especially the plan of being married and having children. In a previous chapter, you've already read that I had many hopes and dreams, and that "my perfect world" included my being married with children as a stay-at-home mother by the age of 27. I had none of these. Because of this, I truly felt numb, worthless and forsaken. It wasn't long before I began to notice that my morning or afternoon runs were becoming a way for me to "cope." I wanted to run away from my life; I wanted to run away from myself.

I decided I needed a "getaway" to the Oregon Coast. The beach for me has always been a location I long for when I need time to myself. Whenever I would tell others where I was going, I would say, "I'm going to go think".

However, when I got there, no thinking happened! Usually, it turned out to be a time to clear my mind as I listened to the ocean waves. Nevertheless, little did I know that on this particular trip God would encounter me there.

As I sat on the beach in silence with my thoughts, I began to experience Him "speaking" to me in a personal, quiet way that rested my soul. Mind you, I had already experienced being filled with Holy Spirit the year prior, and even then, I didn't know that He "spoke". The experience I had there on the beach, listening to God speak to me, was truly unique and beautiful. It was the beginning of a personal and intimate relationship with God. I got a glimpse that day of a personal God and His great love for me, and I wanted more.

What I have come to learn and know is that God is always speaking. He truly wants to tell us so much, but we are often lost in our own worries and desires and distractions that we forget or neglect to really listen. Take me for example, I had been filled with Holy Spirit, yet I didn't know that God spoke since I had been so caught up and worried about my desires and what I thought my future should look like. My prayer for you as you read my story is that you come to hear Him sooner in life than when I did.

Eyes Opened

"I pray that the eyes of your heart may be enlightened, so that you will know what is the hope of His calling, what are the riches of the glory of His inheritance in the saints," Ephesians 1:18

Even when I had reached my low point when shouting my questions into the air, I had no idea that God was really hearing me. I had no idea that He wanted to be known and that He wanted to love on me. I had no idea that I was questioning God Himself. Scripture tells us that God is love. *"The one who does not love does not know God, because God is love."* 1 John 4:8 and *"And we have come to know and to believe the love that God has for us. God is love, and the one who remains in love remains in God, and God remains in him."* 1 John 4:16. Though I unknowingly questioned God, He heard me and He had been faithful to answer my questions. I sit now in awe and wonder to know that He is Love. It amazes me to this day that it was Him that I questioned that day.

Soon after my trip to the Oregon Coast, I began reading my Bible consistently. About three months later, I came across this verse: *"...for God sees not as man sees, for man looks at the outward appearance, but the Lord looks at the heart."* 1 Samuel 6:17. For God to answer the cries of my heart when I hadn't been aware of this verse is proof that though we may not know the Word, God acts on what His word says. God sees the heart of people!

This makes me joyful now when I think about it. You see, when I cried out into thin air, The Lord of Hosts, King of Kings, God Almighty, Jehovah, Jesus, Love, was the One who heard me because my cry came from my heart! It came from the depths of my being because I was in desperate pursuit of answers.

The following scripture is another beautiful promise of His that came into play that day, and again without my knowledge of this verse at the time: *"You will seek Me and find Me when you search for Me with all your heart."* Jeremiah 29:13. I had possessed a Bible, yet even before I began reading it, I had acted on His word and promises! As I began to read the scriptures and hear God speak to me, I began to experience what my heart had been truly searching for—that I mattered, that someone out there loved me, that I was loved, and I felt loved.

Seeking Truth

"Call to Me and I will answer you and tell you great and incomprehensible things you do not know." Jeremiah 33:3

Something that I have come to love about God is that even when we don't know Him or acknowledge Him, and even when we turn our backs to Him, He is always speaking. The part that keeps me in awe of His great love for me is that even when I didn't know scripture, His word was still in action. It always is. His word is a firm foundation, always working. Fortunately for me when I had no idea that His word said the following: *"Call* *to me and I will answer you and tell you great and in-comprehensible things you do not know,"* Jeremiah 33:3, He still remained FAITHFUL to keep His own word and promise to me.

My friend, if you are needing revelation, if you are seeking truth, if you are looking for answers, call to Him. He is faithful even to you, whether you know Him or not. I didn't know Him, yet I called out from my heart and He answered. He will do the same for you.

God speaks in many ways, sometimes with pictures or concepts in dreams, in visions, through people, signs, numbers, the stars, even nature. In the Bible, it mentions where He even used a donkey to relay a message. One primary way that God speaks to me is through dreams in my sleep. I will share one in a later chapter. But please pay attention to your dreams. Job 33:15-16 says, *"In a Dream, a vision in the night, when deep sleep falls on people as they slumber on their beds, He uncovers their ears at that time..."* and Joel 2:28 says, *"After this, I will pour out My Spirit on all humanity; then your sons and your daughters will prophesy, your old men will have dreams, and your young men will see visions."* God is a great communicator, but we are the ones who are horrible at listening. We need to be still and listen.

Revelations

In that season of my life, God began to pour out revelation after revelation to me. I don't know what your path or walk of faith has been, but let me tell you, God started revealing to me how real the spiritual realm is. He started to show me how real His word is and that it is truly alive and breathing. He showed me the great and mighty things I knew not of. Such as how angels and demons are real. And how even newborn believers who have Jesus in their heart, have authority over the darkness: "*Look, I have given you the authority to trample on snakes and scorpions and over all the power of the enemy; nothing will ever harm you.*" Luke 10:19. These were Truths He was revealing to me, and it was only the beginning.

I still had to learn how to walk in these new Truths, but to do so, the wounds in my heart had to be removed and the purity of heart had to be restored. I had to let go of a lot of pain in my heart that clouded my vision of God and the Love He has for me. I will share more about how to do this in a later chapter. The only way one can walk in our authority that Jesus gave us is by knowing and believing that we are fully loved by God, the Creator of the universe "*...who is above all and through all and in all.*" Ephesians 4:6.

Chapter 6

Hole In My Heart

"Now these three remain: Faith, Hope, and Love. But the greatest of these is LOVE." 1 Corinthians 13:13 (HCSB)

Another storm to navigate: I was now turning 30. After the wonderful and beautiful discoveries began in my relationship with God, you might be asking, "Why does the age of 30 matter?" Well, remember a couple chapters ago when I mentioned how the enemy had come in and told me that I would be unwanted if I wasn't married yet by the age of 30? Here I was being confronted with a deadline that paralyzed me with the notion that my time was expiring, and I couldn't stop the clock. As my 30th birthday approached, my greatest fear was staring me in the face. By this time in my life, I had come to know that God was real, that He loved me, yet I *still* felt I was in utter despair over the course and events of my life that I wanted to accomplish. This caused me to become extremely frustrated which led to anger and a re-opening of the wound of feeling forsaken, uncared for, and unwanted. I began to feel as if I was a used-up tissue that had not even been tossed in the garbage where it belongs, but rather tossed on the ground and trampled on.

I felt like God was teasing me. I suddenly found myself feeling that he was some kind of God who always got his way while not caring about people's needs, hopes, fears, or dreams. As if he was a commanding God without compassion regarding the things that matter to us. Have you ever felt like this about God? I felt like a puppet, an empty puppet that was just existing in life but not really experiencing the life I was meant for. I knew that I was meant for great things, for a life of significance, yet everything about the circumstances of my life seemed to say otherwise.

I had a faith that was quickly extinguishing, and a hope that seemed to be failing me, yet I was missing the greatest and most important factor which was an unfailing Love that to my knowledge still didn't exist. A perfect love that reached for me and embraced me in every area of my life. This seemed to be a figment of my imagination.

As my 30th birthday approached, I said to myself, "Well if I am going to be miserable, I might as well be miserable in paradise!" So, what did I do? I booked myself a flight and hotel for Hawaii to "celebrate" my birthday—or more like to forget, and distract myself, and escape my reality. Here is the funny thing: this trip allowed me to cross a few items off my "Bucket List", or

I should say my "Dream List". While it's true that I had "moments" of having my pity parties during the trip, I did have a good time. I went snorkeling and parasailing. I tried amazing food like Ahi Burgers, coconut prawns and malasadas. And I got to sit on a beautiful sandy beach, listen to the ocean waves, and watch the sunset. It truly was a great time in paradise. Yet the entire time there, I felt it—I felt the hole in my heart; I felt a void. Though I was in paradise (and it truly was amazing), I felt as though I shouldn't complain, and that I had so many things to be thankful for. I wasn't thankful at all. Though it was a "perfect experience", I was still missing what I always wanted. Someone to share it with. A man, a boyfriend, a husband. And here I was still single. The truth is, I idolized the idea of having someone to love me. I idolized romance and love. I wanted to be loved, and here I was alone in paradise. Alone... single...unwanted. I could hear those three words echo in my mind.

It didn't really register how deep this void was until about two weeks after I got back from my trip. I was still living with family – a brother and his family. My brother's home had a fireplace and two fire pits out-doors—he enjoys building fires! On one particular day when no one was home, I started dwelling on how my life was a disappointment and how I felt rejected, and still thinking that love didn't exist. I got enraged, and the bitterness rose up in me. I ended up grabbing one of my journals. This was a special journal where I wrote down all my dreams, hopes, and desires for life. With tears flooding my eyes and streaming down my cheeks, and fury coming out of me, I ripped out every single page of this journal. In one of the fire pits outside, I built myself quite a little fire and fueled it with all of my disappointment and anger. I even grabbed my pocket-sized dream list that I carried with me everywhere I went, and I threw that in the fire as well.

All I could say is that I had called it quits. I had had enough of this dreaming and of having high hopes for my life and future. It seemed as if I was not worthy of good things, and that I might as well stop fighting. I had already been through a long season of many, many tears falling on my pillow when I would pray to God and ask Him to just take me home. I wanted Him to take me away from life on this earth and just take me out because, in my mind, there was no point of my being on this earth any longer. I continued to feel that I was of no significance. I felt rejected and thought that no one would even miss me if I were gone. I just wanted to die.

At this point, the scripture that says, *"Where there is no vision, people perish."* Proverbs 29:18 KJV, and this became a reality for me. Oh, I was perishing alright! I let everything inside of me just die! No matter how hard I tried to keep my dreams alive, the fear and rejection from my past still seemed to be bigger.

At that point, I began just going through the motions of "following Jesus" and "doing" His commands. It felt more like I was taking orders from "the boss"—and I was developing an attitude! I wasn't being a friend to The

One true friend who gave the ultimate act of Love for me, who laid His own life down for me. (John 15:13). My mind understood this, yet my heart could not feel it. I was not experiencing His Love and I didn't understand why.

Truth Be Told

It was five months after my epic act of "destroying my dreams," when I decided to attend a new church. That first Sunday standing in worship, I remember hearing someone on the worship team at the microphone saying, "There are some of you that do not believe the power of God's Love." It was as if God had spoken that statement directly to me, and I immediately replied with a degree of attitude. "God, I *do know* that your love is powerful," I retorted back. This brief exchange of conversation that I had just had with God lingered in my mind.

In the worship team member's statement, there was a key word that would take me almost a year later to grasp. That word was "believe." You may have noticed that in my retort, I told the Lord that I "knew" His love was powerful. In the beginning of this chapter, I mentioned that "I had come to know that He loved me". **There is a huge difference between "knowing" and "believing."** Please take a moment to let this sink in. Upon this moment of revelation for me, I felt incredibly "called out" so-to-speak, and so convicted for my instant assuming reply to

God. There is such a stark difference between *knowing* that God's Love is powerful and *believing* in the power of God's Love. This is a "going-from-the-head-to-the-heart" journey.

This is a journey you are also on. A journey that we are all on, whether we acknowledge it or not. The beauty of this is that you are not alone. The enemy wants you to believe that you are alone. He wants you to believe that you are the only one who is unlovable, the only one whose shame "cannot" be removed, the only one who "cannot" be redeemed. I am here to tell you that this is a huge lie. John 3:16 tells us, that *"God so loved the world that He sent His one and only Son so that whosoever believes in Him shall have eternal life."* The key word here is "whosoever!" Whosoever is me! Whosever is *you*! Whosoever is *any person*—any person regardless of their past, regardless of failure, regardless of mistakes. None of these keep us from this Love which is so powerful that it gives us new life, and life to the fullest. The moment you believe in God's Love for you, it changes you! This journey is worth it.

Confession of His love

This revelation for me came in the spring of 2019, in my prayer time on the floor of the living room in my brother's home. It began with me on my knees, sobbing during my time with God. (By now you probably know one thing about me, I cry a lot.) What had made the flood gates of my heart open and eyes fill with tears was when I heard myself declaring out loud to God the things that my heart was learning and beginning to *believe* about Him and His Love.

Here in the living room during a heartfelt prayer for others, I heard myself saying, "...because Your love, God, is truly powerful, and it is the *only* thing that breaks every chain, it truly conquers evil and destroys fear...." As soon as I had spoken those words, suddenly the conversation exchange that I had had with God on the first Sunday in church came back to my mind. In that moment, I realized the powerful difference from what the mind *knows* and the heart **believes**!

"For it is with your heart that you believe and are justified, and it is with your mouth that you profess your faith and are saved." Romans 10:10

Though that scripture talks about our salvation, it also pertains to faith and believing. It is when we profess with our mouth that we are justified. I remember feeling an overwhelming sense of approval from God, and also feeling as if I had finally passed a test! My heart and my mind and my words *finally* had come into alignment with what God had been trying to tell me all along about His Love. Hearing myself speak out loud, I could hear how much I really do *believe* that love does exist, it does conquer evil, and it has power, and it really does overcome! I could hear the answers coming out of my own mouth, answers to the all the cries of my heart that I had shouted into the air!!

This had been such a journey for me—reaching my low point in 2015, God revealing to me how real the spirit realm is, God proving how real and personal He is, and now He was revealing the most important thing I have come to know and the most important thing we all long to believe: that His Love is real, that His Love is true, that His Love is all powerful and beautiful. This revelation did not change my life overnight, I still have had to learn how to walk it out; but He made a point to make it known to me, and He will do the same for you. He doesn't love me more than you. He loves you just the same, with an abundance of love.

Desire Fulfilled

Know this Truth: His Love is the only thing that can change us. It is so powerful and is the only thing that can mend a heart. It breaks bondages, breaks strongholds, breaks chains, and even casts out all fear. Everything that had held me back, Love truly broke through.

The void—that longstanding hole in my heart—got filled with the Love of God when I finally surrendered to it, when I finally confessed it to be real. When Love came in, the mending of the heart began, causing fear to leave, causing rejection to leave, causing the trauma to be healed. This Love is the desire fulfilled. The hope in my heart was now complete. His love in my heart is what made me whole again, it caused my heart to beat again with life!

I shared in chapter 2 that there is hope for you. Proverbs 13:12 was the verse used in the beginning of that chapter.

"Hope deferred makes the heart sick, But when the desire comes, it is a tree of life." Proverbs 13:12 (NKJV)

Throughout this book, I have mentioned that you might be wondering how is it possible for me to have "desire fulfilled" since I am not married yet? With marriage being my greatest desire, how would it be possible for me to experience "desire fulfilled?"

Simply put, the void and hole in my heart that I had was from not being *fully* loved—*all of me*. What God revealed to me was that as human beings, we ALL have an innate desire—a desire from our birth—to be loved. I had replaced the desires that God gave me at my birth with a desire to be married, thinking this was how I would feel fully loved. I thought that once I got married, THEN I would be loved and be made whole. I kept feeling the disappointment and anxiety that marriage wouldn't happen. I now fully know that I am loved by God even though I don't yet have a husband!

When I turned wholeheartedly to God, my God-given innate desire to be loved *was fulfilled*.

All I needed was to believe and receive. I needed to believe that I was fully and completely loved already by the God of Love, the God who is Love (1 John 4:8). I needed to believe that I was already Loved by Love himself.

And maybe this is where you are at, too? Maybe you desire to be loved; maybe you are waiting on a spouse; maybe you have put your hope on your family, children, friends, church, alcohol, drugs, sex, work, business, money, being healthy, working out, trying to "fill" your void, your God-given desire to be loved. Brother and sister, please take the time to stop at this very moment and breathe. Know and believe that God has already poured out His intense, unending love for you through His Son Jesus at the cross so that we can be loved by God for the rest of our lives.

It is only God's love that will fill this hole in your heart and make it whole again. He is *near the broken-hearted* (Psalm 34:18), He is faithful to mend and restore your heart; even more, He will turn it into a tree of life, just as He did mine!

Chapter 7

Perfect Love

"There is no fear in love; instead, perfect love drives out fear, because fear involves punishment. So that one who fears has not reached perfection in love." 1 John 4:18 (HCSB)

I was finally believing that God is all of who He says He is, that He loved me, that He truly cares about all my heart wounds, and that He has a plan for me! I knew that I was beginning to be perfected with new understanding about God and how He was operating in my life. He then began teaching me about perfect love.

At this point, you might be pondering, what is perfect love? I cover more about this a bit later in this chapter, but briefly, perfect love is Jesus, perfect love is God. As I mentioned before, God *is* Love. Love is a powerful action with intention and choice, but love is also something that we all seek, something that will fill our hearts and make them whole again.

I looked up the definition of love. One definition says that "it seeks the welfare of all." In short, it is a selfless act! Another definition I kept finding is "affection." Per Merriam-Webster Dictionary, the first definition of affection is "a feeling of liking and caring for someone or something: tender attachment." I want to draw your attention to the "caring" portion of the definition since "being cared about" is primarily what I had wanted to feel—to feel loved and accepted by someone who I knew cared about me.

God cares *so much* about you and me. He cares so deeply about our lives, our well-being, and our hearts. He is intricate, detailed, and complex. I could share story after story about how personal He is and how He has been in my life even in the smallest of ways, and I would like to share one of those experiences with you now.

After I had told God that I was finished with my dreams and that I would bury them, I was still quite bitter and angry when I began attending the new church where the deep Love of God was frequently discussed. On that first day when I had retorted to God, there was also a time during the worship service when another team member took the microphone and directed us to put our right hand over our heart. They continued by saying that God wanted to revive dreams that were buried. I'll tell you, at first, I was not thrilled to hear this—I am just being honest. Now that I look back, I can see that God was simply being intimate and caring about what my desires are. He doesn't want our hearts to be heavy, sad, hurt, or even hardened.

He truly does care about our heart and our heart's desires. Hear me again—heart's desires, not worldly desires. He cares so deeply that He will use others to speak into our lives. He wants to heal the hurt and wounds that caused our hearts to become hardened so that we can receive more than what we ask for—and we can be grateful, not entitled. He cares about you.

The Power Of God's Love

God's Love is so perfect and powerful that it casts out fear! There have been many amazing truths that God has revealed to me regarding His love for me. The first is that the opposite of fear is *not* faith. So many times I have heard the phrase, "Your faith has to be bigger than your fear," which I was never able to agree with wholeheartedly. What God pressed on me and taught me is that in order to remove fear, there is only *one* thing that can do that. That is Love—perfect Love, which is His Love.

Don't get me wrong, you will undeniably need faith, but to cast fear out, love is what will do that. The Word of God says that *"perfect love cast out fear."* 1 John 4:18. In the New Living Translation which speaks so much to me, it says, *"Such love has no fear, because perfect love expels all fear. If we are afraid, it is for fear of punishment, and this shows that we have not fully experienced his perfect love."*

Faith will most certainly be needed in this process. Scripture says, *"faith is the substance of things hoped for, the evidence of things not yet seen."* Hebrews 11:1. And it also says that *"without faith you cannot please God."* Hebrews 11:6. This is an important truth to grasp.

Hear me out. When it came to my hope, all the actual dreams and desires were not the things that I thought I hoped for most. What I desired most was a single overarching hope which was to be truly loved. This overarching hope pointed me to Jesus. Early in my journey, God gave me Psalm 27:4, *"I have asked one thing from the Lord; it is what I desire: to dwell in the house of the Lord all the days of my life, gazing on the beauty of the Lord and seeking Him in His temple—(His presence)."* He used this scripture to speak to me, and it began to stir me to seek Him, it whispered to me that He has the answers and that He has everything I could ever possibly need.

Another revelation for me in this Love journey was in learning the connection with 1 John 4:8 *"God is love"*, and 1 John 4:18 *"perfect love drives out fear"*. Since God is love, it takes faith to place our hope in God's Love, believing so greatly that He loves us that we are unquestionably convinced that He will come through for us and that He will not let us fall. Our hope then is rooted in love. We then allow God's Love to guide us, and when we do, fear is cast out.

Another wonderful thing is that this Love—His love—is the only thing that will remove the wounds, the hurt, the pain, the anger, the bitterness, the rejection, and the disappointment in our heart.

His love is *that* powerful! Love comes in and restores every single area making it whole again and bringing it back to life. Our hearts start beating to a new song of joy. That is what God's Love can do. It is what He will do for you if you receive it, just as He did for me.

Perfect Love Revealed

God gave me a dream that helped me understand just how powerful His love is.

Here was my dream:

I was scratching my right lower back with my right hand when suddenly I felt a dry and scaly organic "thing" on my back. I also began to see and feel this scaly entity on my left shoulder. It was diagonal across my back, from the top left shoulder down to my lower right back. I somehow knew that it was yellow in color and that what I had touched was some kind of large parasite. I then saw four of these smaller parasites of different colors on the back of my left hand. I was able to remove the ones on my hand by "peeling" them off with my right hand. When I peeled them off, the top layer of my skin was torn off with them, but it did not cause bleeding.

End of dream.

The dream interpretation:

The scaly parasites represented burdens, demons, generational curses, strongholds. The smaller ones on my hand were less serious, superficial, and easily removed—which was why I was able to peel them off with my hand. The authority of a "believer" can easily remove these, and I operated in my authority. However, the parasite on my back represented a larger and deeper issue, and the fact that it was on my back indicated that the issue was something persistent. The color yellow represented the spirit of fear. The parasite on my back was a stronghold of fear that brought nothing but death and lifelessness to my life.

Through this dream, the stronghold I had in my life was exposed and revealed to me. It was now time for the fear to be removed once and for all.

Pressing into the dream:

When we get a dream that doesn't make sense and we still have questions, it is always best to go to God and press in until we get the answers. I can hear some of you asking, "How do you press in?" and, "What do you mean by pressing in?" What I mean is while asking God questions, press in to hear Him speak to you and earnestly seek answers. (In the next few paragraphs, I will share with you what I did to press in regarding this dream.)

I was so intrigued by this dream that I wanted answers. For about three hours while working at my office,

I persistently let my mind and thoughts press in. I remember going into the bathroom to find a private place to pray in tongues and create a space for a breakthrough. I knew the importance of pressing in, and God often speaks to me when I begin to pray in tongues. It was vital that I ask for answers and breakthrough, and that I asked intently even though I was at work. I crave His voice and presence.

The biggest question that remained unanswered for me after this dream was "How do I remove that disgusting pest on my back?" Though it wasn't on my back physically, I knew it was truly on me in the spirit realm. It gave me the heebie-jeebies just to think about it so I wanted it gone! What transpired next was a conversation I had with God in the bathroom at work that went as follows:

Me: "God, it is physically *impossible* for me to remove that thing off my back. Can YOU PLEASE remove it? Give me a vision of your hand coming down and You peeling it off my back."

God: "No, Maritza."

Me: [in a desperate plea] "Excuse me? Why not? God, it needs to come off!"

God: "Maritza, I won't do that because removing it would rip off chunks of your flesh since it is deep into your bone. If I were to do that, it would kill you."

Me: (Walking back to my desk, fighting back tears, I sit and keep talking to God). "Well, Lord, will you *help* me? Help me with what I need to do? Lord, I don't want this thing to be on me."

God: "That thing is causing lifelessness in you. Maritza, what gives life?"

Me: (Fortunately, I had read scripture that week that gave me the answer). "Umm... blood, God—blood carries life."

God: [staring at me with a ginormous smile on His face as He lets me think]

Me: "The Blood of Jesus!"

God: "Correct. Now apply that to your back and on your life."

At this point I got up from my desk, I went back into the bathroom and into the stall. I closed my eyes and just envisioned the Blood of Jesus being poured on my back. What I saw next was incredible! This "thing" on me did NOT like THE BLOOD! It started letting go of me! It had tentacles that had gone into my flesh and wrapped itself around my spine and as the Blood of Jesus was poured on me, the ugly parasite started to remove itself and release itself from me. It was as if I was a hot potato to it! It wanted to get *rid of me!* I saw it release and un-attach itself from my back and fall off of me. My flesh intact, my skin was smooth and healthy.

Talk about Perfect Love casting out fear! Amen and Hallelujah!

WOW! What this Love can do! God's Love is so powerful it expels all fear! And fear appears in *many* different ways.

A book that helped me break more strongholds of fear off my life is: Destroying Fear by John Ramirez. This was a book that made me realize that fear can also be in the form of insecurity, anxiety, and isolation. I saw that the fear in my life came from a lot of rejection. And let me tell you, rejection is an ugly thing to deal with, and Love is the only way to break that. For the longest time I felt like I never belonged anywhere—not in my family, or in my church, or in other social events. I did not have a problem socializing, that is for sure, but I never felt like I belonged. It was not until this Love, this genuine perfect love of God, was poured into my own heart that I was able to receive the genuine love of others.

What is this Perfect Love?

"Love is patient, love is kind.
Love does not envy,
is not boastful, is not conceited,
does not act improperly,
is not selfish, is not provoked,
and does not keep a record of wrongs.
Love finds no joy in unrighteousness
but rejoices in the truth.
It bears all things, believes all things,
hopes all things, endures all things."
1 Corinthians 13:4-7

This scripture gives us a description of love, a way to know what love looks like. And what I really want you to grasp is that the spilled and poured out Blood of Jesus IS this perfect Love. Jesus willingly made a choice to allow his life to be sacrificed for us, a choice to go to the cross to redeem us, a choice to be tortured and crucified in order to make every wrong *right* between us and God. The Word also says that *"There is no greater love than to lay down one's life for another."* John 15:13. That scripture is exactly what the Blood of Jesus represents—His choice to shed His blood, to give his life for you and me. This is the ultimate act of sacrificial Love.

YOU ARE LOVED

We all need to grasp that we are absolutely Loved beyond measure, this includes you. Simply put, God so deeply loves you that He gave His one and only Son for you—his name is Jesus. And when the moment in time arrived, Jesus willingly made the decision to go to the cross *for you.* I will repeat that again, Jesus made the decision to go to the cross for YOU! He sacrificed Himself *for* you. And by accepting His sacrifice of love for you, you may not only have eternal life, but you may experience His love now so that your heart may fully be restored and you may live again!

If you have never received Jesus as your Lord and Savior, this is the perfect time for you to accept and receive

Him. There is no better time to receive this perfect Love in your heart. He has already paid the price and He calls you "Loved and Accepted". If you want to know and experience this Love that He has already poured out for you, now is the time to receive it. You don't have to go to church or perform any kind of ritual. All you have to do is speak to Him from your heart. If you do not have the words, you can say something like the following:

Jesus, I am sorry for the sins in my heart that have kept me apart from you. I am sorry for the things I have done wrong against You. I am sorry for seeking love in ways that are not rooted in You. I open the door of my heart to You; I choose to believe You and make You Lord of my life. I choose Your Love and I choose life. Thank you for what you did for me on the cross, and thank you for your spilled out love for me. Fill me with all of your love and fill me with your Holy Spirit. In Your mighty and precious name, I pray. Amen.

Welcome to the best journey of adventure you will ever have! This is a journey of discovering your purpose and living the life you were meant to have, full of the goodness your heart desires—LOVE, peace, and joy!

Chapter 8

Confidence In Love

"I belong to my love, and His desire is for me" Song of Solomon 7:10 (HCSB)

Honestly, I believe we need to read that scripture out loud. Okay, let's read it again and I want you to let it sink in before you read any further. *"I belong to my love, and His desire is for me"* Song of Solomon 7:10. Meditate on this, allow each word to become real to you, and let it come alive.

Take the time to let your soul and spirit be drenched in that scripture. This is a scripture that really spoke to me and helped me walk in confidence, knowing that The God of Love *keeps me, loves me, and helps me.* Belonging to someone gives a sense of security and purpose. Please hear me, YOU BELONG to the God of Love and He wants the best for you!! He wants to show you great things and give you joy.

I do wish that this scripture had been given to me long ago. I even wish that I had heard about the Love of God early in life. The reality is, what I have gone through helped me discover and experience True Love, and to be able to share about it with you—and for all of that, I am grateful.

I actually didn't find this scripture until after having a confidence in Love. "Discovering" it further solidified my faith in God's Love for me and has further anchored my belief that He truly wants the best for me. Sometimes we must step out in faith to discover that God does not fail us but rather indeed wants and has the best for us beyond what we can dream, ask, or imagine (Ephesians 3:20). It is only after we have stepped out that we find the abundant blessings of God.

When we start walking confidently in this Love, amazing things start to happen. Wonderful experiences you never imagined and opportunities to do things you never thought you would! It is different for everyone so it's important not to compare. For me, once I began to walk in this confidence, doors started opening. I began to write, and let me tell you, I never imagined I would do this. Since I was in high school, I have disliked writing. Then I found myself traveling to countries I didn't even know existed! This is how God works. When you finally get into a place where you don't overthink or over analyze anything, He leads and takes you to places beyond what you could have thought of. I also have found myself speaking on stages sharing about the Love of God. Weeping with a heart full of gratitude, I realized that I was being used to speak into people's lives and to give hope to them. This was beyond me indeed. I know that for some of you reading this, this might freak you out a little bit. You might be thinking "I would never do that," or "I could never do that." Listen, God's grace comes in with help along with His love. When you grasp the Love He has for you, you will do anything for Him, and you will want others to come to know this Love.

Walking in Love

Now that you have learned that God loves you, that you belong to him, now what? Well, this is where we walk it out afresh each day. We learn to walk in this Love. We walk knowing the God of Love is always with us. You are a royal beauty, walking along hand in hand with your King, stately and secure. **We walk knowing that we are loved and protected, walking in confidence that nothing can harm us any longer.** Walking in a confidence where no fear can reside any longer, only Love.

Walking in God's Love also means living life in such a way where the love we have received from God overflows and is poured out to others, i.e., we begin to want to love others, too. *"Therefore, be imitators of God, as dearly loved children. And walk in love, as the Messiah also loved us and gave Himself for us, a sacrificial and fragrant offering to God."* Ephesians 5:1-2. I ended the previous chapter with the "Love" scripture passage of 1 Corinthians 13: 4-7 that explains what love is, but I believe it is crucial to also let the verses in Ephesians 5:1-2 seep into your heart and soul. In short, Love is this: to lay down your life for others. *"This is how we have come to know love: He laid down His life for us, we should also lay down our lives for our brothers."* 1 John 3:16. Wow! I know it's hard to imagine, but can I say that once you have received the knowledge of His Love—the revelation of Him—then this walk of love starts to pour out of you in such a way that you can't even comprehend. Just like Ephesians 3:19 says, it is a *"love that surpasses knowledge."*

This overflow of God's love is *the perfect bond of unity* (Colossians 3:14). It is what allows us to live lives full of peace and harmony with everyone else, including with ourselves. Loving ourselves is something many people struggle with, men and women alike. Truth be told, this is something that needs to happen before we can love others. When Jesus was asked what the greatest commandment is, He replied: *"Love the Lord your God with all your heart, with all your soul, with all your mind, and with all your strength. This is the first and greatest commandment."* However, Jesus didn't stop there. He continued by saying, *"The second is equally important: Love your neighbor as yourself, there is no other commandment greater than these."* Mark 12:28-31. This command has two-in-one that go together—loving God first, and before we can love our neighbor we must first love ourselves.

If you are struggling with loving yourself, draw close to God. James 4:8 says, *"Draw near to God and He will draw near to you."* He is the only one who will be able to speak into those places where you don't feel you can love yourself. He will help you see yourself the way that He sees you and this will change how you think about yourself and how you see yourself. Even now, I pray in the name of Jesus that He starts changing your perspective of how you see yourself. Remember that God made you in His image: *"Then God said, 'Let Us make man in Our image, according to Our likeness...'"* Genesis 1:26. God does not create junk. You, my friend, are wonderful, beautiful, worthy and valuable.

Walk Worthy and Fully Loved

"Above all, put on Love, the perfect bond of unity." Colossians 3:14

This is an instruction; it tells us to put on Love. This sounds so simple yet we over- complicate it. I absolutely love how Ephesians 4:24 says it: *"You put on the new self, the one created according to God's likeness in righteousness and purity of the truth."* We are to clothe our new selves with Love, righteousness, and purity. We put these on as our royal robes to wear every single day and we walk worthy of the Love we have received. We walk as royalty in this love, confidently, knowing whose we are. And knowing that the King above All is the One who loves us, and fights for us, and who showed us his love for us by laying down his life first. That right there makes me smile, and I hope you realize the truth in this as well!

So, whatever it is that you are going through even at this moment, my hope for you is that you come to learn more about putting on this love. This love that is already yours. To not look at circumstances, nor mistakes, or the past, but to look at the One who has already laid down His life for you, who says you are righteous, holy, blameless, and pure. Put this mantle on you. Put it on knowing you are a rightful heir. We are co-heirs with Jesus, which means that we have the right to put on everything He is. Jesus laid down His life in Love, to give you His. The great exchange. Our dirty rags, for His white pristine robes. I have gone from a place of having a heart full of trauma, of hating myself, of being bitter, disappointed, angry, depressed, hopeless, to a heart full of life, joy, peace, dancing, laughter, singing and I am excited to be alive again, all because of *this* Love. I am fully restored. This is also available for you!

I can't emphasize enough just how amazing this love is. It truly is better than *any other*. A most perfect love, most wonderful in which God truly cannot lie to us. He is the perfect person to provide love because His love NEVER disappoints. You will get lost in His love, you will only want more and more of it.

My Ending Prayer for You

"...I pray that you, being rooted and firmly established in love, may be able to comprehend with all the saints what is the length and width, height and depth of God's Love, and to know the Messiah's love that surpasses knowledge, so that you may be filled with all the fullness of God." Ephesians 3:17-19

Atmosphere Of Love

Creating a safe place in your heart to receive love

This section holds treasures that I would like to share with you that helped me to be loved by Love. These may help create an atmosphere in your heart for allowing love to sink into places that you didn't even know existed. You may find that these help "break your heart open" as they did for me. Whether they help you or not, these are for you to enjoy.

The declarations in here are personal journal entries from when I was beginning to allow the Love of God to come into my heart, and entries of my awe of His Love.

There are also songs that speaks about God's Love that helped me press in further. And other songs that seeped deep into my heart and soul, soothing away every pain I had carried. I enjoy worshiping the Lord, and these songs have been very impactful in allowing my heart to open more to the Love of God. Our praise and worship are weapons against despair.

My experience of His Love:

His Love is the only thing that can break bondages and change us. As I learned more and sought Him more, He showed me that He wanted to work in me. By giving me Psalm 27:4, He told me that He wanted me to just let go and to learn to allow HIM to just love on me.

I look back and, yes, it was scary. It was so scary to allow someone to love me, to truly love me, because love is so powerful. But God is Love. He is perfect and can never let us down. He is the safest person we can allow to Love us. He is faithful and cannot lie, He loves to love us, and give us grace, and He is full of mercy. HE makes us beautiful in His Love.

Journal Entry 8/29/2018: This is what He was telling me, but insert your name

"(Name), let Me just love you. When you worship, let Me just love you. When you just are, let Me just love you. Rest and let Me just love you. Don't think about anything and just soak in My presence, in My love. I want to hold you and love you. Let me hold you. Stop thinking about what to do, just let Me love you."

Lord, our hearts yearn for you but some of us are afraid to let go.

Let go of what?

Pain?

Bitterness?

Fear?

Shame?

Frustration?

Why?

It is easier to hold on to this and to blame others or circumstances. To not take possession of our land (our heart). It is what we know, it is familiar.

Lord, for the hearts that are crying for You, soften them. Let us open our hearts to You, to Your love so that it may cast all unclean things out.

Help us let go, help us let go of these things that keep us from You. These things that hold us back from You and from our true selves in You. The things that keep us from your love.

Remind us of our desire to be with You, in You always, to be in Your presence, to seek You, to gaze at Your beauty, Lord. Remind us that You are our focus. And when we let go in order to focus on You and allow You to love us, ALL is well. Because You are holding us, because You are protecting us, Your love is healing us, Your love is perfecting us in your image, Your love is empowering us, your love is making us whole, Your love is purifying us, and

You Oh Lord keep us and Fight for us as we rest in your love.

Thank you Jesus, praise You Jesus.

Journal Entry 9/1/2018: I Let you Love Me

Let you Love me.
I will let you Love me, Lord.
I will let you Love me,
I will let you cleanse me.
I will let you perfect me
I will let you love me
I will let you
I will let you make me whole, Jesus
I will let you love on me
I will let you love on ALL of me
I want you to love me
I want to be in your Love, Lord
I want you to pour your love on me.
I want you, Lord Jesus
I want you
All I want is you
All I desire is you
You are the only one I desire, Lord
It is what I desire, to be in your love and in your presence every day, every hour, every second of my life, Jesus.
To know you, to know your love; So I say Lord, I WILL LET YOU LOVE ME
I will let you love me, I let you, Lord.

Journal Entry 11/30/2020: To Be Loved By Love

There truly is nothing like being loved by Love
It is breathtaking
It is wild
It is overwhelming yet blissful
It is joyful
It is pure
It is warm yet invigorating,
Or should I say exhilarating.
Lord to be loved by Love
To be loved by You.
Truly nothing compares. Nothing.
It is the most powerful thing to be loved by You.
To be loved by Love.
Being loved by Love
I find my peace
I find my self-worth
My whole being is restored.
Being loved by Love
I am complete, made whole
Being loved by Love
I am confident and bold.
It is how I become firm and unshaken.
Being loved by Love every false thing is shattered,
All the lies are obliterated, and I stand.
My whole being is what is left.

Being loved by Love
Only a lovesick smile would be found on my lips.
My eyes twinkling
Lost in wonder
Heart at peace.

Declarations

I am fully and completely Loved
I am known
I belong
I am worthy
I matter and my life matters
I am capable
I am strong
I am smart
I am intelligent
I am whole
I am joyful
I am victorious
I am wise
I am more than enough
I am valuable
I am the righteousness of Christ.
I am confident
I am beloved
I am wanted
I am fruitful
I am an overcomer

Love Songs

Your Love is Strong, by Cory Asbury
God is Love, by Chris Renzema
Reckless Love, by Cory Asbury
Love Song, by Jonathan David Helser
Here I am, by Chris Renzema & Moriah Hazeltine
I am Loved, by Mack Brock
Lean Back, by Capital City Music, Dion Davis
Beautiful Things, by Gungor
Revival's in the Air (God of Love), by Bethel Music
Melissa Helser
Closer, by Maverick City Music, Brandon Lake
I Could Sing of your Love Forever, by Shane & Shane
Love Has Won, by Citizen Way

Forgiveness

If you are struggling with forgiving yourself, or forgiving anyone for that matter, here is something to help you. The list starts with forgiving yourself and I mention a few common areas. But I also pray that Holy Spirit will come to you right now and remind you of areas or struggles or people that are not mentioned on this list.

This is verbiage to help you. Say out loud:

Jesus, I forgive myself ...
For hating who I am
For blaming myself
For being ashamed of myself
For being ashamed of my past
For being ashamed of my family
For being angry
For rejecting myself
For doing _____ when I knew I shouldn't have
For not loving myself

And Jesus, I ask for Your forgiveness and I thank You for Your forgiveness.

About The Cover

God told me He wanted two purple hearts for the cover of this book, and when I inquired with Him about this, He reminded me about the Purple Heart medal that is presented to military service members who have been wounded or killed as a result of enemy action. God told me, "You are in a battle and you have been wounded." I asked Him, "Why *two* purple hearts?" He responded, "The second one is mine, for I too have been wounded."

In awe, I recalled how Jesus truly was wounded unto death.

The larger heart that has light radiating from it is His heart, and His love is restoring life to the other heart. Which is your heart and mine!

CPSIA information can be obtained
at www.ICGtesting.com
Printed in the USA
LVHW080007111221
705839LV00006B/14